Cinderella
and
The Sleeping Beauty

Retold by Rose Impey
Illustrated by Peter Bailey

ORCHARD BOOKS

Cinderella

Imagine, if you can, a young girl whose mother died, leaving her to be brought up by her father. She was a pretty girl, with a kind nature exactly like her mother's, so father and daughter lived together very happily, until the day that he decided to marry again. But then everything changed.

This time the man chose a different

Cinderella
and
The Sleeping Beauty

For Siân
P.B.

Orchard Books
96 Leonard Street, London EC2A 4XD
Orchard Books Australia
Unit 31/56 O'Riordan Street, Alexandria, NSW 2015
The text was first published in Great Britain in the form
of a gift collection called *The Orchard Book of Fairy Tales*
illustrated by Ian Beck, in 1992
This edition first published in hardback in 2000
First paperback publication in 2001
Text © Rose Impey 1992
Illustrations © Peter Bailey 2000
The rights of Rose Impey to be identified as the author
and Peter Bailey to be identified as the illustrator have
been asserted by them in accordance with the
Copyright, Designs and Patents Act, 1988.
A CIP catalogue record for this book is available from the British Library
ISBN 1 84121 564 3 (hardback)
ISBN 1 84121 574 0 (paperback)
1 2 3 4 5 6 7 8 9 10 (hardback)
1 2 3 4 5 6 7 8 9 10 (paperback)
Printed in Great Britain

type of wife entirely, the most conceited woman you ever saw, with a sharp tongue and a temper to match. Soon he was completely under her thumb.

The woman already had two daughters, unpleasant, spoilt creatures like herself, so she resented her stepdaughter's sweet nature and set out to make the girl's life as hard as she could.

This is how she did it. She gave her own daughters the best bedrooms and made her stepdaughter sleep in a draughty attic. She dressed her own daughters in fine clothes, while her stepdaughter's clothes were little more than rags.

She left her own daughters to do as they pleased, which was usually nothing, but she made her stepdaughter work hard cleaning the house and waiting on her stepsisters.

To make matters worse, when her work was done, the only place the girl was allowed to rest was beside the fireplace, in among the cinders. And so she became known as Cinderella, the cinder girl.

But, despite all this, Cinderella grew more and more beautiful – far more beautiful than her sisters with their fine clothes and fancy manners. And this made them even more envious of her.

Now, as it sometimes happened in those days, the king's son decided to hold a Grand Ball, and an invitation soon arrived for Cinderella's stepmother and her daughters. For the next week they talked of nothing else. They couldn't decide which clothes they should choose, what hairstyle to have, which jewellery to wear, how to make up their faces – and all this made more work for Cinderella. Yet the harder she worked for them, the worse they treated her.

"Wouldn't you like to go with us?" they asked Cinderella.

"Oh, yes," she said. "If only I could."

"What a pity she can't," said one.

"Yes, it doesn't seem fair, does it?" said the other.

"Poor Cinderella," they said.

You might have thought they meant it, if you hadn't noticed how they smiled at one another, then burst out laughing, as if it was the most ridiculous suggestion in the world.

Cinderella was used to their unkindness, but that didn't make it any easier to bear.

At last the important day arrived. When the rest of the family was ready they climbed into the carriage and Cinderella watched as they drove away. Then, alone in the house, she finally broke down and sobbed at the unfairness of life.

And it *was* unfair.

But one person cared about Cinderella and hated to see her upset, and that was her godmother. When she found the girl crying she said, "Oh, my dear, whatever's wrong?"

"I just wish…" Cinderella began. "If only I could go…" But she knew she couldn't. There was no point wishing for the impossible.

However, her godmother was a wise woman with fairy powers. She knew what Cinderella wished for, and nothing was impossible to her.

"You *can* go to the ball, if that's what you want. Do exactly as I tell you and we'll see what we can manage. Now go into the garden and find me a pumpkin."

Cinderella went straight away, though she couldn't begin to see how a pumpkin was going to help. She brought back the largest she could find. Her godmother scooped out the middle, then touched it lightly with a magic wand.

Only a tap, the slightest touch, nothing much, and it became an elegant coach, covered with gold.

"Well, that's a start," said her godmother. "But a coach without horses won't go far. Bring me the mousetrap."

Again Cinderella
did as she was told.
Inside were six grey
mice. She lifted the
trap door. One by one
the mice ran out. But once
more her godmother was
ready with her wand.

Only a tap, the slightest touch,
nothing much, and the mice turned into
six fine horses, harnessed and ready to go.

"A coach without a coachman isn't a great deal of use," said her godmother, looking around as if she expected to find one in the kitchen.

"The rat trap!" suggested Cinderella.

In it they found a big fat rat with long whiskers.

Another tap, only a touch, and he changed into an amiable coachman, without a sign of a tail.

"Better and better," said her godmother. "Now, into the garden again.

You'll find six lizards hiding behind the watering can. Bring them to me."

Cinderella brought them in.

A tap and a touch and six smart footmen in gold livery jumped up behind the coach just as if they'd been doing it all their lives.

"Now," said her godmother, "are you ready to go?"

Cinderella looked down at her clothes. She hated to seem ungrateful but she could hardly go to a ball dressed like this.

The lightest tap, the gentlest touch, and she was dressed in a gown of gold and silver. The slippers which stood ready for her to wear were made of glass, sparkling crystal. There has never been a pair to match them. Cinderella put them on. A perfect fit.

Looking exactly like a princess, she stepped into the coach.

But her godmother had one more thing to say. "Promise me you will leave the ball before midnight. One moment after twelve and your coach, horses, coachman and clothes will disappear. You'll be just as you were."

"I promise," said Cinderella. "I won't forget." It seemed to her a small price to pay. She thanked her godmother and waved goodbye.

When Cinderella reached the palace, her arrival was announced and the king's son himself came out to meet her. As he led her into the ballroom, the music and dancing stopped. The prince and Cinderella began to dance. She looked so graceful that at first all the other guests sat and watched.

"Who is she?" everyone wanted to know.

"Certainly a princess," they whispered.

The whole evening she danced only with the prince; he wasn't interested in anyone else.

At supper she sat close by her sisters and once or twice spoke to them. They were very flattered and answered her politely. They didn't recognise her: people usually see what they expect to see, and they hardly expected to see their own sister dancing with the prince.

All too soon the clock struck quarter to twelve. Cinderella remembered her promise. She curtsied and left.

When she reached home, Cinderella told her godmother all about the ball and asked if she could go again the next night. The prince had begged her to come. As they were talking, Cinderella heard her sisters arrive home. She hurried to let them in.

"It's very late," she said, yawning and rubbing her eyes, as if she had been asleep.

"You wouldn't have noticed if you'd been with us," they said. "We've had the most wonderful time. A beautiful princess came to the ball. She spent almost the whole evening talking to *us*."

"Who was she?" asked Cinderella.

"Nobody knows, but the prince is desperate to find out. You should have seen her clothes…"

"I wish I had," said Cinderella. "Perhaps tomorrow I could go too."

"You! Whatever would you wear?"

"I could borrow a dress from you," she suggested.

"Lend a dress to a cindergirl? Don't be ridiculous," they said.

They were quite sure she must be joking, as of course she was. Cinderella didn't need *their* help.

20

The next day, as soon as her sisters had left, Cinderella began to get ready. This time she wore a dress of deep blue silk, covered in jewels that sparkled like stars in the night sky. And again she wore her glass slippers.

The prince was waiting for her when she arrived. Throughout the evening he didn't leave her side. He was determined she wouldn't slip away from him again.

Cinderella was so happy and excited that she didn't once think about the time. That's how easily promises are forgotten. Before she could believe it, the clock began to strike midnight.

One! Two! Three! In panic Cinderella fled from the ballroom.

Four! Five! Six! She ran down the steep staircase. She could hear voices and footsteps, but she didn't dare to look back.

Seven! Eight! Nine! Running across the courtyard she stumbled and lost one of her glass slippers, but there was no time to stop.

Ten! Eleven! *Twelve!* By the time Cinderella was clear of the palace she was again dressed in rags. All the magic had vanished, all except one of her glass slippers. She took it off and hid it safely in her pocket.

The prince had tried to follow Cinderella, but he couldn't catch her. He only found her other glass slipper, lying on the ground. He questioned the palace guards; she must have passed them.

But they said they'd seen no one. They didn't imagine the prince would be interested in a poor girl dressed in kitchen rags.

Cinderella reached home just in time to open the door to her sisters as they returned from the ball. She asked them if the beautiful princess had come again.

"Well, she did," they told her, "but the moment it struck midnight she disappeared. She ran off into the night, with the prince chasing after her."

"He came back clutching her slipper," said one.

"Obviously madly in love," said the other.

"Do you really think so?" Cinderella asked.

"Oh, yes," they both agreed. There was no doubt about it.

And they were right. The very next day the prince announced that he would marry the girl whose foot fitted the glass slipper.

First it was tried on by all the princesses, then the duchesses, then all the ladies of the court. You should have seen the variety of feet. Some had big feet and some had small feet, but none were small enough to fit the tiny slipper. So that was a mystery.

Then it was taken into every home in the land. At last it was the turn of Cinderella's sisters to try it on.

Well, they squeezed and they squashed their feet to get the slipper on. They pushed and they pulled until their fingers ached They trapped their toes and hurt their heels and made them bleed, but it was no use. They had to give it up.

By now the prince was beginning to lose all hope. "Isn't there anyone else in the house?" he asked.

"No other *lady*," they said. "There's Cinderella, but she doesn't count."

Immediately the sisters wished they'd held their tongues, because the prince insisted they bring Cinderella and let her try it on.

The moment she sat down and took the slipper, they saw how easily it slipped on, how perfectly it fitted. And when she took from her pocket the matching slipper and put that on too, they were speechless.

The prince recognised her, even in her rags. And when her godmother appeared and once more, with only a tap, the slightest touch, transformed Cinderella's clothes, even her sisters saw that she was the beautiful princess from the ball.

Then they were afraid, and regretted how they had treated her.

"Do forgive us," they begged her. "We're truly sorry."

Cinderella did forgive them, because that was her nature. And soon after, when she married the prince, she took her sisters to live at court, where they met two great lords. These two were an equally proud and unpleasant pair, so when they married they made a good match. All four of them lived miserably together for many long years.

But as for Cinderella and the prince, now they lived happily ever after, which was exactly what they deserved.

The Sleeping Beauty

In the days when there were still
fairies, there lived a king and queen
who were immensely rich. They lived in
a magnificent castle with servants,
golden coaches, and everything that
money could buy, so they should have
been happy, but they weren't. All the
money in the world couldn't buy what
they wanted: a child of their own.

One day, when the queen was walking beside the castle, she found a fish on the riverbank. It had thrown itself completely out of the water and lay gasping and close to death. She quickly lifted it back into the river and so saved its life. In return the fish told the queen, "Within a year your dearest wish will come true." And sure enough, as the fish had promised, the queen gave birth to a baby girl.

When the child was born the king was the happiest man alive.

He held a great feast to celebrate and decided to invite all those fairies who lived in the kingdom. Now the fact was, the king only owned twelve gold plates and there were thirteen fairies, so he was forced to leave one out. This proved unlucky for the king, as you will see.

After the feast the fairies gathered around the child's cradle. Each gave her a gift: beauty, wisdom, grace and many other virtues.

Finally it was the turn of the twelfth fairy. But before she had time to speak, the doors of the castle flew open and in came the thirteenth fairy – the one who'd been neglected. She was dressed entirely in black and was in such a rage that everyone shrank in fear as she passed.

Standing before the child's cradle, the fairy cried out, "Since you chose to ignore me, this will be my gift: when the princess is fifteen she will pierce her finger with a spindle and drop down dead." Then the fairy turned her back on the baby and left without another word.

The king and queen looked all around in despair, but no one knew how to console them. But the twelfth fairy, who still had to speak, offered them some hope.

"Although I cannot undo the curse," she said, "at least I can soften it. The princess will not die, only sleep for a hundred years."

A hundred years! This was small comfort to the king. He was determined to protect his daughter if he possibly could. He made a law banning the use of spindles throughout the kingdom, and he ordered that those which already existed should be burned. Only then did the king and queen feel secure.

Over the years all the other gifts were fulfilled. The princess grew up beautiful and good, just as the fairies had promised, so that whoever met her couldn't help but love her.

One day, when the princess was fifteen, while the king and queen were out riding, she began to explore parts of the castle into which she'd never been allowed. She discovered a derelict tower, and climbed the winding staircase to the very top. There she found a door; in the lock was a golden key.

She turned it and the door opened to reveal an old woman sitting, spinning flax.

"What are you doing?" asked the princess, because of course she'd never seen a spinning wheel in her life.

"Spinning," said the old woman. "Here, you try." And she handed her the spindle.

The instant the princess touched it she pricked her finger and three drops of blood appeared. She fell into a deep sleep.

Very soon the king and queen returned from riding, followed by their servants, and the enchantment descended on the castle like a fine mist.

One moment life was going on as normal. The kitchen maid stirred the soup and the butler poured the wine for the king's dinner. The kitchen boy,

turning the spit to roast the meat, stole
a tempting scrap for himself, and the
cook, catching him in the act, reached
out to cuff his ear. But the next
moment they all stopped – just like that
– and fell asleep where they stood.
Even the fire over which the meat was
cooking died down and seemed to rest.

No one escaped, not even the animals: the horses steaming in the stables, the dogs fighting in the courtyard, the doves cooing on the castle roof, the flies resting on the kitchen wall – all suddenly fell asleep and everywhere was silent and still.

Around the castle a hedge of thorns appeared, deep and impassable, and so high that only the tallest turret could be seen above it. It wrapped itself around the sleepers like a thick blanket, keeping everyone inside safe and undisturbed.

For years afterwards stories of a beautiful princess who lay sleeping inside the castle were often repeated. A succession of young men came from distant countries hoping to find a way inside, but the hedge always defeated them. No matter how fiercely they fought a way through, the hedge always grew back again, thicker and sharper, catching them in its thorns. Many of them lost their lives in the struggle.

But one day a king's son was travelling through the kingdom and was told the story by an old man who lived nearby.

Immediately the prince knew that he too must try. The old man reminded him of all the others who had been equally convinced they could succeed, but had nevertheless perished in the thorns. But the young man was determined.

Now it happened that the hundred years came to an end on that very day. As the prince approached the hedge, it parted magically before him and offered a clear way through, then closed again behind him.

The king's son walked on until he came to the courtyard, but there he almost gave up at the sight of so many lifeless bodies.

The silence was unbroken even by the buzz of a fly; the still air unruffled by the slightest breeze. Such a strange atmosphere made him almost lose his nerve, but he made himself go on. As he came closer, he could see that these were not dead, but sleeping bodies, overcome in the middle of their daily business. Some snored gently, others smiled as if dreaming pleasant dreams.

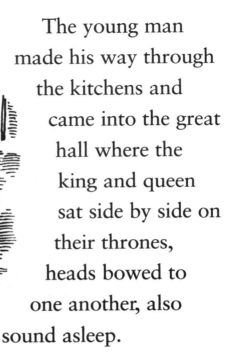

The young man
made his way through
the kitchens and
came into the great
hall where the
king and queen
sat side by side on
their thrones,
heads bowed to
one another, also
sound asleep.

And still he kept on and at last
came to the top of the tall tower where
the Sleeping Beauty lay. When he
looked down on her and saw that she
was as beautiful as he had heard, and
even more beautiful, he couldn't resist
bending over and kissing her on the lips.

And so the enchantment was broken
and she awakened.

"How long you have been," she
said and smiled up at him.

And suddenly everywhere was life
and noise and confusion. The king and
queen woke hungry from their deep
sleep, and called for their dinner.

The cook caught the kitchen boy by the ear and advised him to keep his fingers to himself, or he'd be sorry.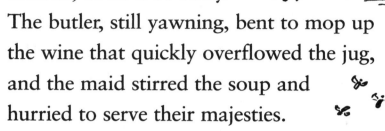

The butler, still yawning, bent to mop up the wine that quickly overflowed the jug, and the maid stirred the soup and hurried to serve their majesties.

The horses in the stable and the dogs in the courtyard set up a racket, for they  too were more than ready to be fed. The doves cooed contentedly and stirred themselves and flies buzzed in every corner of the castle.

Then the Sleeping Beauty and her prince came down from their tower to announce their wish to be married. The wedding was arranged within the week. After a hundred years asleep everyone was highly excited at the prospect of a royal wedding. It was, after all, exactly what they had been waiting for.

HANS CHRISTIAN ANDERSEN TALES FROM ORCHARD BOOKS

RETOLD BY ANDREW MATTHEWS
ILLUSTRATED BY PETER BAILEY

1 **The Emperor's New Clothes and The Tinder Box**
   1 84121 663 1   £3.99
2 **The Little Match Girl and The Wild Swans**
   1 84121 675 5   £3.99
3 **The Little Mermaid and The Princess and the Pea**
   1 84121 667 4   £3.99
4 **Thumbelina and The Tin Soldier**
   1 84121 671 2   £3.99

Orchard Fairy Tales are available from all good bookshops,
or can be ordered direct from the publisher:
Orchard Books, PO BOX 29, Douglas IM99 1BQ
Credit card orders please telephone 01624 836000
or fax 01624 837033
or e-mail: bookshop@enterprise.net for details.

To order please quote title, author and ISBN
and your full name and address.
Cheques and postal orders should be
made payable to 'Bookpost plc'.
Postage and packing is FREE within the UK
(overseas customers should add £1.00 per book).

Prices and availability are subject to change.